THE

CHRISTMAS

LOON

This book is dedicated to the people that made this book possible. My mother Dorothy, Jim and Joanie, Mac and Dorothy, and Gramma Pearl.

Designed by Tom Martinson

ISBN 1-55971-092-6

NorthWord Press, Inc.
Box 1360 Minocqua, WI 54548

ACKNOWLEDGMENTS

Many people helped this book become a reality. My best friend Jan and my three children deserve the most credit. Bob Anderson and Gary Olson helped me obtain many of my favorite photographs. Others, including Gary and Linda Moss and Frank Dickson made important contributions. My brother Jim provided me with film when I couldn't afford it. A thank you also goes to the long list of people who helped but are too numerous to mention here.

THE
CHRISTMAS
LOON

Tom Martinson

NORTHWORD
PRESS, INC.
BOX 1360 MINOCQUA, WI 54548

My name is Jenny.

I live with my mother and father in a cabin on a big lake in the Great Northwoods. I have an older sister Katie and an older brother Andy. I love to play with them.

Sometimes Katie and Andy stay after school or sleep at a friend's house. Then my mom says, "You have to learn how to play by yourself." I try but I get lonely and I don't have any fun.

I was in the first grade at school. There was only one week before summer vacation started. I didn't want school to end because I knew I wouldn't see my friends as much, and I knew I would be left at home without Katie and Andy again. I had lots of fun when Katie and Andy were home but not when they were gone.

When we got home from school on the last day, my mom had made a special dinner for us. My dad was a teacher so he was on vacation now, too. I asked my mom, "What are we going to do tomorrow?" "I'm going to take Katie to gymnastics camp and Andy is going fishing with the Johnsons for a week. You and Dad can stay home and relax," my mom said. I tried not to cry, but it was hard.

Then Dad said, "You and I can get up early and canoe around the lake." I burst into tears and left the table and ran outside. I watched the sunset, thinking that my whole summer was going to be terrible.

The next morning my dad woke me up at 4:30. It was still dark. I had never been outside in the morning before the sun came up. I got into the canoe and looked around as my dad pushed us out into the water.

The dim light turned the rocks and trees into different shapes that were kind of scary.

It began to get lighter and lighter. I saw colors I had never seen before. First purples and blues, then pinks and reds, and then oranges and yellows. I was glad my dad had gotten me up early for this.

As the sun rose higher, it turned the water into a bright gold color. "Let's paddle around and see if we can find something else to look at. There's something," he said, as he turned the canoe and headed for what looked like a little dot on the water.

As we got closer and closer, I asked, "What is it?" My dad whispered, "It's a loon."

It was the biggest and prettiest bird I had ever seen. It was all black and white with big red eyes!

As we drifted closer, the loon swam in front of us into the golden water, then went headfirst into the water and was gone. It almost seemed like it had never been there at all.

"Can we get close again?" I asked. "No, we better leave them alone for now," my dad said as he paddled slowly away. "You mean there's more than one?" I asked.

"Yep, the other one is probably sitting on their nest." "Nest?" I asked. "Yep, in two or three weeks they'll hatch one or two chicks." "Chicks?" I asked. "Yep, on a lake this size there is room for only one pair of loons and they raise one or two chicks each year."

"Can we go look at the nest?" I asked. "No, if we want to look at the nest we should get my telescope so we can see the loons without disturbing them. Otherwise they might leave the nest and the eggs and never come back," my dad explained.

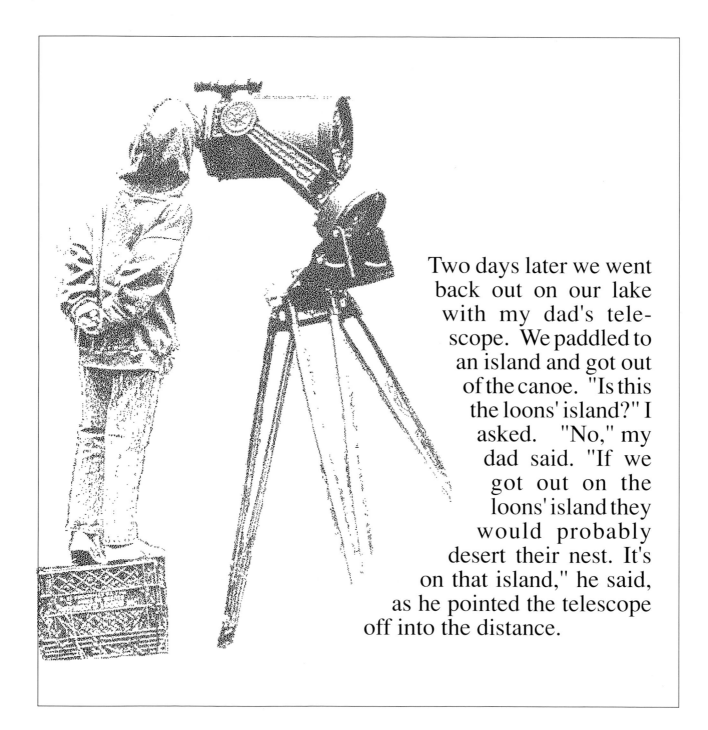

Two days later we went back out on our lake with my dad's telescope. We paddled to an island and got out of the canoe. "Is this the loons' island?" I asked. "No," my dad said. "If we got out on the loons' island they would probably desert their nest. It's on that island," he said, as he pointed the telescope off into the distance.

He looked through the telescope and then said, "There it is," as he moved over to let me look.

I didn't know what to expect, but when I looked through the telescope, the big bird seemed to jump out at me. It was beautiful!

We took turns looking through the telescope. Soon the other loon came to take its turn at sitting on the eggs.

As the one loon left the nest, we could see two eggs. The other loon pushed its way onto the nest and before it sat down, it turned the eggs over with its bill, "to make sure the eggs don't get any cold spots," my dad said.

As we got into the canoe, I asked, "Where do the loons go when they're not sitting on their nest?" "I think they go and eat," my dad said. "They dive under the water and catch fish and crayfish. Their red eyes help them see underwater."

As we paddled our way home, we glided around an island, and there was one of our loons with a big fish that it had just caught. It tipped its head back and swallowed the fish.

"Dad, when will the eggs hatch?" I asked. "It takes about 29 days for loon eggs to hatch once they are laid. Our eggs were probably laid awhile ago so they should hatch in a week or two. If we check every couple of days we might be lucky enough to see the chicks on the nest." We checked every two days and even though the eggs didn't hatch then, we had a lot of fun.

We would always go out early and sometimes we would see moose,

or deer with velvet antlers,

or a hen mallard with ducklings, hiding along the shore.

We always saw something that made us glad we had gotten up early. My summer vacation had been just great.

Then one day when I looked through the telescope, I saw something I hadn't seen before. A little head was sticking out from under the loon's wing. The loon eggs were hatching!

When the other loon came back to sit on the eggs, we got to see what the little chick looked like. It looked like a little gray ball of fluff.

The other egg hadn't hatched yet. "The other egg better hatch soon," my dad said. "Sometimes loons won't wait for both eggs to hatch, especially if something scares them."

The next morning we were on the lake before sunrise. It was foggy, but as the sun peaked above the trees we saw our loons. But where were the chicks?

Then we saw them, one and then two little chicks riding on the backs of the adult loons. "Why do they do that?" I asked. "They stay warmer when they're out of the water," my dad said, "and the chicks don't have to waste any energy trying to swim along with their parents."

The loon parents fed the chicks minnows, insects, and crayfish.

Just about every time the adults would dive, they would come up with some food for the chicks.

The chicks would try to dive
like their parents but would
pop back up to the surface.

My dad and I watched our family of loons throughout the summer. Our favorite time to see them was always right before the sun rose. Our family of loons somehow made our lake complete. Without them, something always seemed missing.

Sometimes early in the morning it was very foggy when we went out in the canoe. Then we would not be able to find the loons until one of the adults would make a very sad noise that is called a wail. I heard the loons make three or four different calls, but the wail was my favorite.

When the chicks were small, both chicks could ride on one
of the parents' backs.

The chicks never seemed to get full and would even eat big cray-fish.

The chicks grew rapidly and after about 10 days they were too big to ride on their parents' backs.

Then they would eat as much as they could,

yawn,

and take a nap.

My dad and I watched our loon chicks grow throughout the summer. They got bigger and bigger until they didn't look like chicks anymore. One chick was smaller than the other chick and this is the chick I liked the best. I thought she was a little girl like me and I named her **Oot**. This is the noise that loons make to tell each other that they are near and not alone.

Oot would always hide behind one of her parents when they traveled around the lake. The way her bill matched the adult loon's necklace made me think that maybe that was the reason why adult loons had the white feathers on their necks.

More and more we saw the young loons without the adults. They could now catch fish by themselves but would still beg for food when their parents were nearby.

Then all of a sudden it was September and I would be going back to school in a few days. I would miss my almost daily canoe trips with my dad to see our loons. I would especially miss little **Oot**.

The first weekend after school started, my dad and I went out on the lake to see our loon family. We found only the two young loons. The only trace of the adults was a single feather that I found floating on the water.

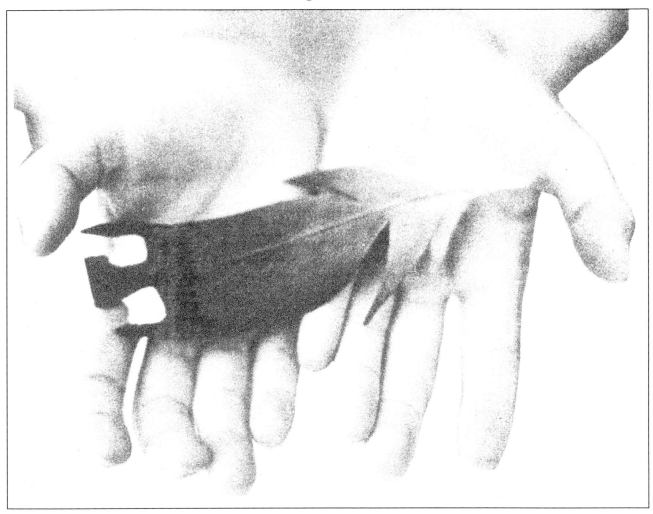

"Now I know how they get all those white spots on their bodies," I said to my dad.

"But where have the mom and dad gone?" I asked my dad. "They have already headed south," my dad said. "I think our loons spend the winter out on the ocean."

"But how do these young ones know where to go?" I asked. "Some birds migrate each year. They know by something called instinct," my dad said. I didn't understand what this meant and it made me more uneasy than ever.

The next couple of weekends passed and our young loons were still on our lake. Then, one Sunday morning we found that only little **Oot** was left. Now I was sure that my favorite loon had been left behind to face the winter alone. I told my dad that we had to do something to save **Oot**.

I had never seen **Oot** fly and it was getting colder every day. I didn't think **Oot** could leave even if she knew where to go.

When Saturday came again, there was snow on the ground when we went to get into the canoe. We found **Oot** looking cold and all alone on our big lake. I called out, "**oot, oot**" and the little loon paddled over toward our canoe, then went down under the water. She came to the surface far away and we paddled back home to get warm.

Sunday morning came with such a snow storm

that we could not go out on the lake to see if **Oot** had flown away.

The next week in school went slowly. All I could think of was **Oot**. Luckily Saturday morning came at last. As my dad and I walked outside, we knew at once that something was different. It was too quiet — our lake had frozen.

Did **Oot** leave? Did she learn to fly? "Do you think she's frozen in the ice?" I asked my dad. My dad tried to comfort me, "I'm sure **Oot** could fly. We just didn't ever see her fly. And I'm sure she left last Saturday after we saw her, just before the snow storm. I'm sure of it. Birds and animals can tell when storms are coming and this was just the push that **Oot** needed. The strong wind proba- bly helped her fly south.   I'm **sure** of it."

I wanted to believe my dad but could he really know for sure? And all of a sudden I felt alone again.

Only this time I didn't feel quite so all alone. I knew my dad cared just like I did about **Oot** and that made me feel a little better.

School kept me busy now, but I still remembered my little loon. Halloween and Thanksgiving came and went and I always had fun, but every now and then I would think of **Oot** and I would feel sad.

For Christmas our family was going to fly to Chincoteague, Virginia to visit my grandparents. My mom showed our family a book about wild ponies that lived on an island near the ocean, not too far from our grandparents' house.

Dad said, "If we get some extra time, maybe we can look for some of these ponies.

The ride in the jet was fun. I got to sit by the window and look out at the land and clouds below. I thought about how much fun summer vacation had been and how much I had learned, but then I thought about **Oot** again and it made me kind of sad.

We landed and drove to our grandparents' house. It was a nice old house and all the decorations made it feel like Christmas. Katie and Andy hung their stockings up by the fireplace but I didn't want to so I said I would later.

I looked out the window and thought about last summer and our loon family.

The next day was Christmas Eve, so mom made us go to bed early. I couldn't go to sleep so dad came and told me, "Even though tomorrow is the day before Christmas, I'm going to give you my present early. We are going to get up early and go see the wild ponies of Assateague Island.

"If you're real good and go to sleep, you'll find your Christmas present there." I didn't understand what he meant, but I did fall asleep.

The next day we got to As-sateague Island early in the morning. I saw birds I had seen before like the Great Blue Heron,

and other new birds like a young mute swan.

And then we saw the ponies of Assateague Island

They were real shaggy and friendly too!

After we watched the ponies for awhile, my dad said, "Come over here and let's see if we can find Jenny's Christmas present." We walked over a big sand dune and for the first time we saw the ocean.

We walked and walked along the beach. I found a big sea shell! Was this my present?

Then my dad stopped and said, "Look over there." Katie and Andy and I looked out over the ocean. We couldn't see anything at first, but then we saw a bird riding the waves out on the ocean.

I looked at my dad. "Is it **Oot**?" I asked. "Is it?"

"Well," he said, "it could be, and now you can see that young loons can migrate to the ocean all by themselves. And even though that may not be our **Oot** out there, I think **Oot** did fly away and she will fly back to our lake someday."

Maybe it wasn't **Oot**, but I waved goodbye just in case.

Well, I believe what my dad said was true, and it was the best Christmas present that I'll ever get. When we got back to gramma's house, I hung up my Christmas stocking.

That night I went to sleep dreaming of Santa Claus, summer sunrises on our lake back home, and little loons fishing out on the ocean.